It's a very special day for Sid today. . . .

"Today is my birthday!"

Sid's favorite birthday treat in the whole wide world is . . . cake!

Do you know what Sid would like on his cake?

"An extra-yummy dinosaur made out of frosting."

Cake-a-licious!

Sid has another super idea:

"Why wait until your birthday to have birthday cake? Why not have cake for breakfast, lunch, and dinner? Why don't parents let us eat cake *all* of the time?"

Just then Sid hears his mom.
"Hey, Sid, it's breakfast time!"
she calls from the kitchen.
"Yippee! It's time to eat!"

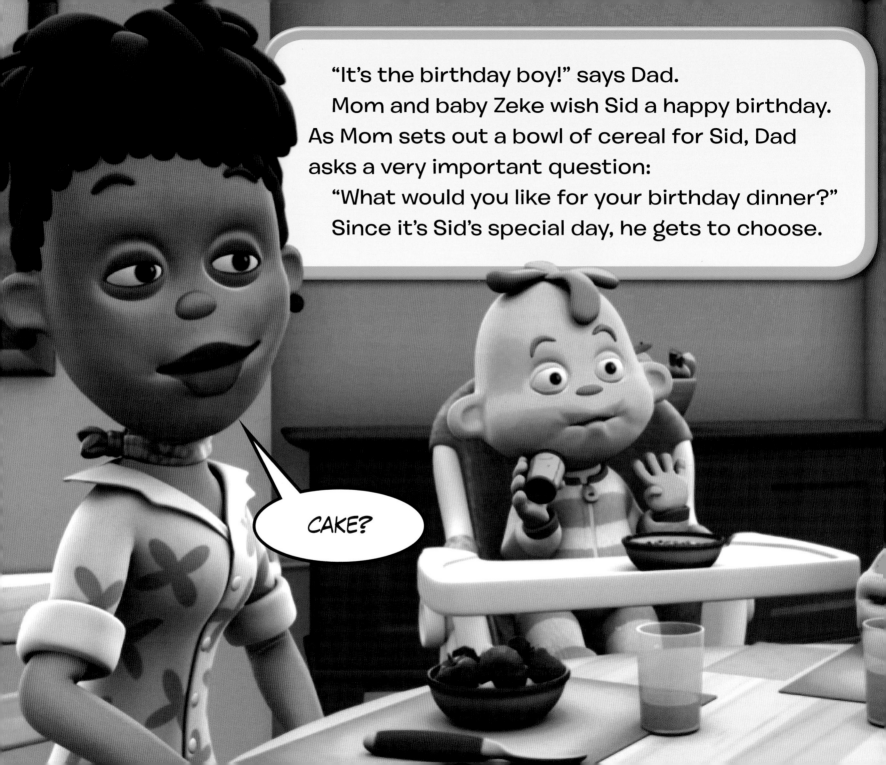

"It's the birthday boy!" says Dad.

Mom and baby Zeke wish Sid a happy birthday. As Mom sets out a bowl of cereal for Sid, Dad asks a very important question:

"What would you like for your birthday dinner?" Since it's Sid's special day, he gets to choose.

CAKE?

The *Let's-Read-and-Find-Out Science* book series was originated by Dr. Franklyn M. Branley, Astronomer Emeritus and former Chairman of the American Museum–Hayden Planetarium, and was formerly co-edited by him and Dr. Roma Gans, Professor Emeritus of Childhood Education, Teachers College, Columbia University. Text and illustrations for each of the books in the series are checked for accuracy by an expert in the relevant field. For more information about Let's-Read-and-Find-Out Science books, write to HarperCollins Children's Books, 10 East 53rd Street, New York, NY 10022, or visit our website at www.letsreadandfindout.com.

Sid the Science Kid: Why Can't I Have Cake for Dinner?
© 2010 The Jim Henson Company, Inc. JIM HENSON'S mark & logo, SID THE SCIENCE KID mark & logo, characters and elements are trademarks of The Jim Henson Company. All Rights Reserved.
Manufactured in China. No part of this book may be used or reproduced in any manner whatsoever without written permission except in the case of brief quotations embodied in critical articles and reviews. For information address HarperCollins Children's Books, a division of HarperCollins Publishers, 10 East 53rd Street, New York, NY 10022.
www.harpercollinschildrens.com

Library of Congress catalog card number: 2010921270
ISBN 978-0-06-185266-4
Typography by Rick Farley
11 12 13 14   SCP   10 9 8 7 6 5 4 3 2
❖
First Edition

LET'S-READ-AND-FIND-OUT SCIENCE®

STAGE 1

Jim Henson's
SID
the Science
KID

Why Can't I Have
Cake for Dinner?

Adapted by Jodi Huelin

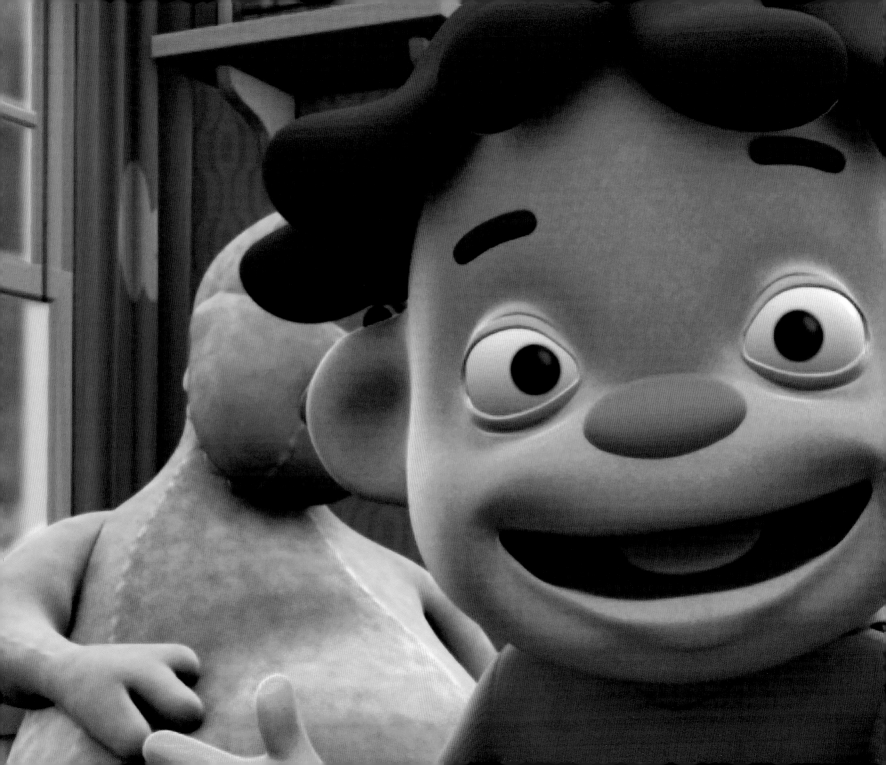

Sid's answer is as simple as it is tasty.
"Cake."
Mom and Dad are a bit confused.
Of course Sid will have cake, but *after* dinner.
Right?

FOR DINNER?

Mom explains why cake is a *sometimes* food.

"Cake has a lot of sugar in it," Mom says.

"How about cupcakes, then?"

"Too much sugar," Mom says again.

"Little cookies shaped like cake?"

Can you guess the answer?

"Too much sugar," Mom says once more.

BUT CAKE IS SO YUMMY!

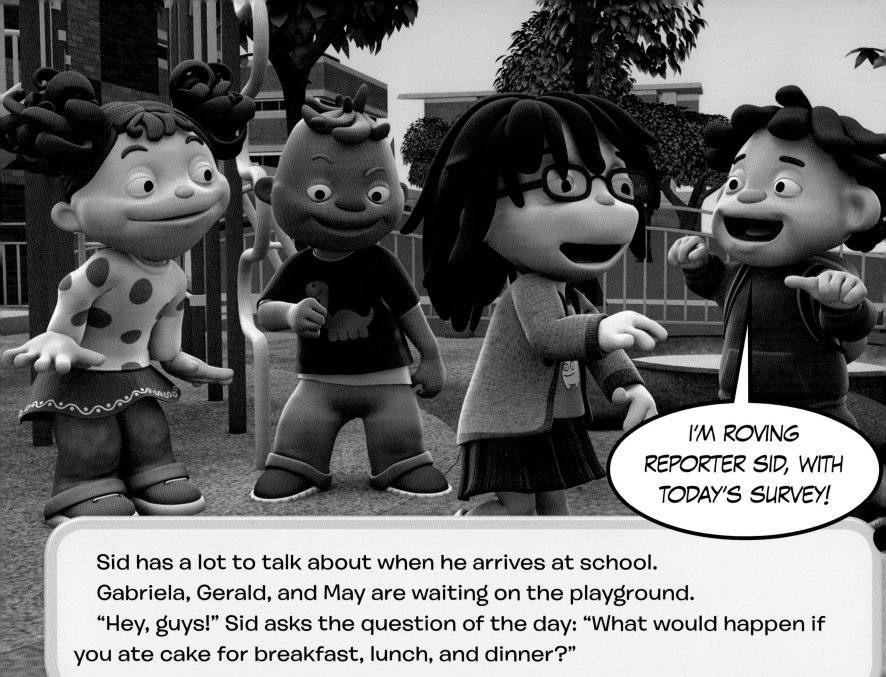

I'M ROVING REPORTER SID, WITH TODAY'S SURVEY!

Sid has a lot to talk about when he arrives at school.
Gabriela, Gerald, and May are waiting on the playground.
"Hey, guys!" Sid asks the question of the day: "What would happen if you ate cake for breakfast, lunch, and dinner?"

"I think your tummy would feel yucky," answers May.

Gabriela explains that Sid isn't the only one who likes cake.

"I once saw a bunch of ants eating cake at a picnic. They liked it, so maybe eating cake all day *is* a good idea."

Gerald tells how lots of cake makes him feel.

"When I eat lots of cake I run around and around . . ."

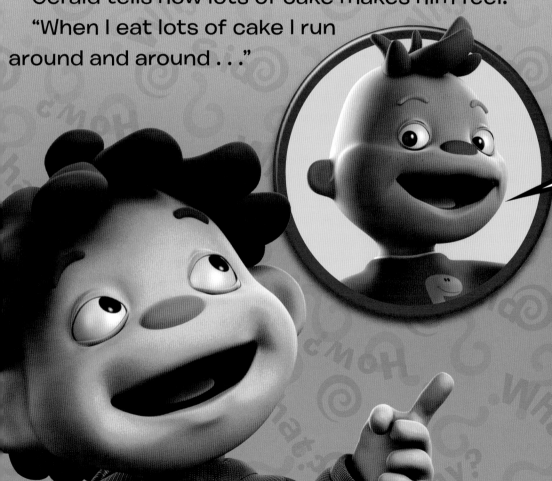

"AND AROUND, AND AROUND, AND AROUND, AND AROUND, AND AROUND . . ."

The kids take their seats.

Before they get started on today's lesson, Teacher Susie has a special greeting.

"Happy birthday, Sid!"

Sid's friends wish him a super-duper-schmooper birthday, too.

"Do you have a birthday wish you'd like to share?" Teacher Susie asks.

Sid sure does.

"My wish is to eat cake for breakfast, lunch, and dinner!"

Teacher Susie agrees that cake tastes good, but says it's not for eating every day.

"Nutritious foods have all the things in them you'll need to grow strong and healthy," Teacher Susie explains.

Is it important to feel healthy?

Sid's friends show him what *they* can do when they're feeling strong and healthy.

Gabriela flexes her muscles.

May whirls and twirls around.

Gerald asks what types of food are nutritious.
"That's a perfect question!" says Teacher Susie.
"Let's explore that at the Super Fab Lab!" she calls.

The kids all grab their journals and their lunch boxes.

Teacher Susie wheels out a big chart.

"The best way to eat a nutritious meal is to eat a bit from each food group every day."

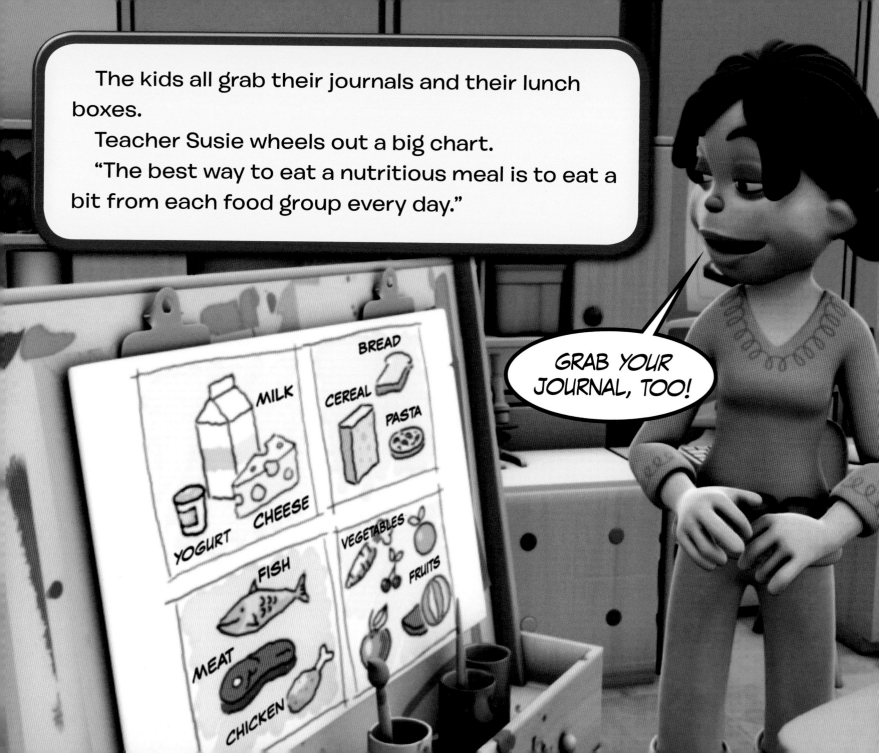

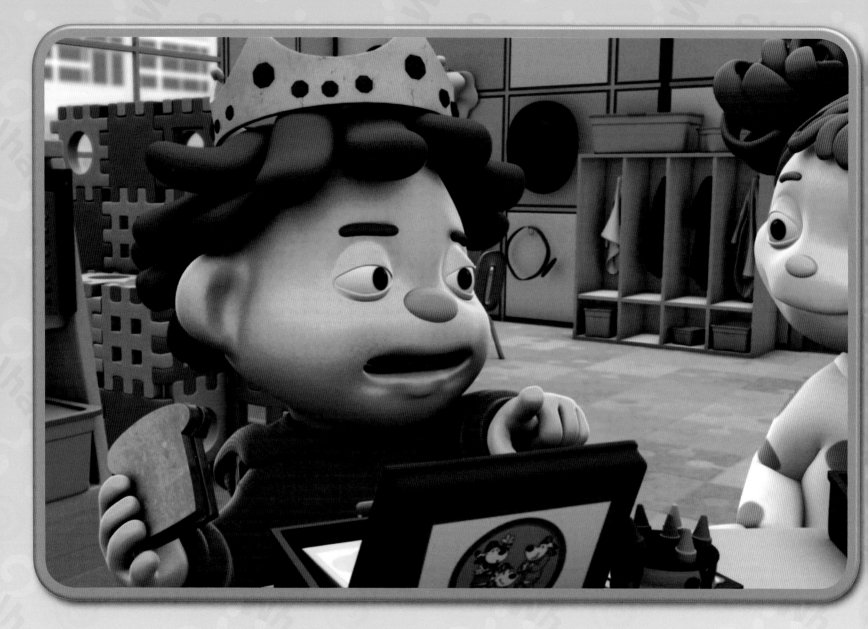

Sid notices something *very* important:

"There's no *cake* on that nutritious food chart!"

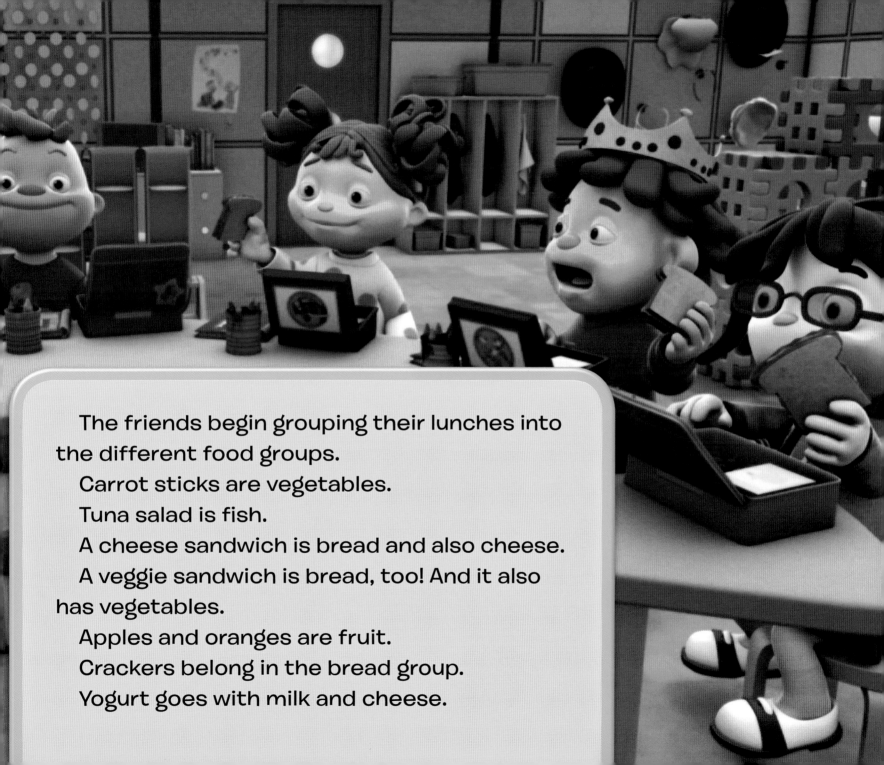

The friends begin grouping their lunches into the different food groups.

Carrot sticks are vegetables.

Tuna salad is fish.

A cheese sandwich is bread and also cheese.

A veggie sandwich is bread, too! And it also has vegetables.

Apples and oranges are fruit.

Crackers belong in the bread group.

Yogurt goes with milk and cheese.

Now it's time to see what's in Sid's journal.
"I drew my nutritious birthday meal!"

Teacher Susie is impressed with each of her scientists. "You know so much about eating healthy, nutritious foods!"

Sid is sad that he can't eat cake all day, but if he did, his body wouldn't be getting enough nutritious foods. If he eats cake only once in a while, and eats a little bit from each food group every day, he'll have enough energy to run and jump and play!

When Sid gets home he knows *just* what to request for dinner.

"I'd like mashed potatoes, peas, a glass of milk, and some of Mom's Jumbo Gumbo."

Hey—those are foods from each food group! He learned about that in school! And Sid got his wish from this morning, too. (But with a nutritious, delicious twist.) A yummy cake with a dinosaur made out of . . .

Teacher Susie showed Sid and his friends the different ways to eat nutritiously. The different foods that you and Sid learned about fit into four "food groups."

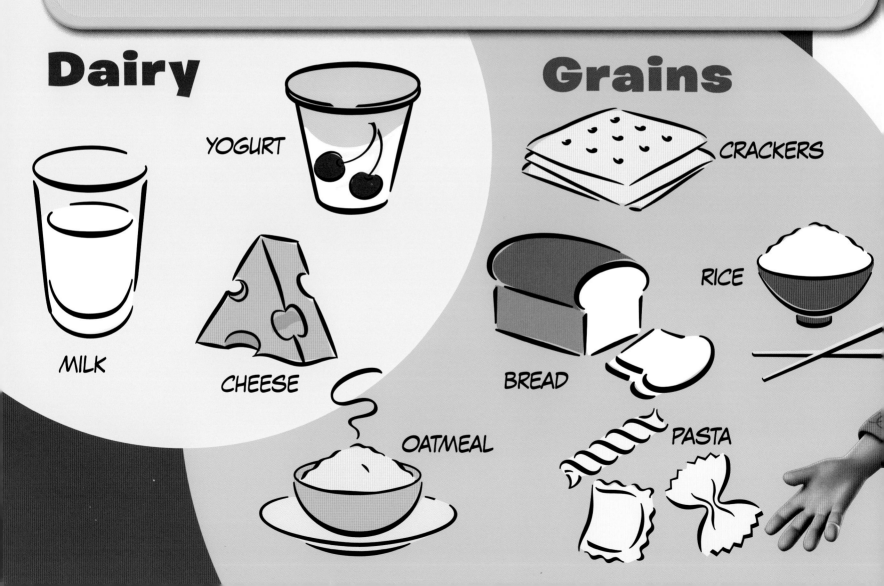

Dairy

YOGURT

MILK

CHEESE

Grains

CRACKERS

RICE

BREAD

OATMEAL

PASTA

Sid the Science Kid's Food Chart

Sid had the choice to eat nutritiously and so do you! Don't forget that not all foods are create equal. On the left you'll see the foods that will help you run faster, jump higher, and have the energ to learn better. On the right are the foods that taste super-yummy but don't have the vitamins and nutrients you need to stay healthy. Those are foods best eaten only occasionally.

All the foods on the right should be eaten only in *moderation*. What's moderation? Moderation means every once in a while—not every day. So even though all those foods on the right are yumm special treats, they're not good for your body, so you should only eat them in moderation.

A-OK!

GREEN BEANS

CHICK PEAS

GLASS OF MILK

BROCCOLI

SPAGHETTI AND
MEATBALLS

TOAST WITH JAM

APPLE

CHICKEN BREAST

PORK LOIN

HUMMUS

OK Sometimes

DOUGHNUT

CROISSANT

CANDY

HOTDOG

PEPPERONI

RANCH DRESSING

MAYONNAISE

REFRIED BEANS

ICE CREAM

CAKE